Stories for 3 Year Olds

Stories
for
3
Year Olds

Jane Riordan
Gabi Murphy

bookoli

Contents

We're Not Afraid of the Dark

The sun had set, it was the end of the day.
A family of squirrels had finished their play.

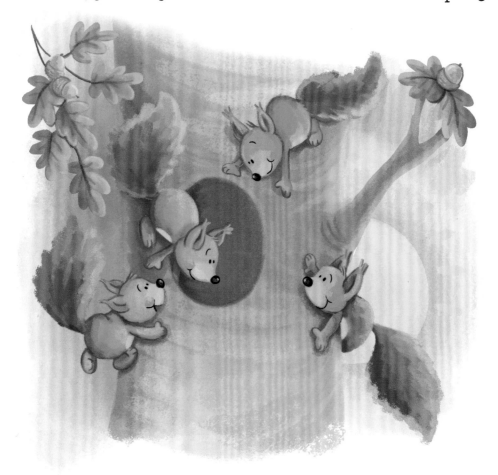

They scampered to their tree and came indoors.
They brushed their tails and washed their paws.

One little squirrel, tucked up in bed.
"I'm not afraid of the dark," he said.

SQUEAK

came a sound from under the house.
The squirrel jumped. "I hope it's just a mouse!"

Two little squirrels, tucked up in bed.
"We're not afraid of the dark," they said.

BUMP went a sound out on the stair.

JUMP went the squirrels. Oh, what a scare!

Three little squirrels tucked up in bed.
"We're not afraid of the dark," they said.

KNOCK

went a sound,
over by the door.
A long, scary
shadow fell
across the floor.

One little squirrel hid
behind her paw.
"I really don't like this
dark anymore."

CRASH went a sound, right beside the bed.
"Oooowww! Oooowww!" a scary voice said.

BANG! BUMP!
Then a big, spooky **BOOM!**
Just as a shadow spread across the room.

But it wasn't a monster at the door.

Just little squirrel
number four!

No wonder she'd
made all that noise!
Her paws were piled
with food and toys.

She'd brought a lamp,
she'd brought some sweets.
She'd brought some fruit,
and other yummy treats.   11

And then the midnight feast began!
Three sat eating; one squirrel sang.

They bounced and bounced and had a pillow fight,
and forgot all about the dark of the night.

Four sleepy squirrels, tucked up in bed.
"We're not afraid of the dark," they said.

"The dark is best for a night-time surprise."
And with that thought, they closed their tired eyes.

I Can Do It By Myself

This is Kitty. She is a fuzzy, furry bundle of trouble! One day, she was busy rolling up a big ball of wool.

"Let me help you," said Mother Cat.

"No! I can do it by myself," said Kitty.

But Kitty was getting in a terrible tangle.

In fact, you could hardly see Kitty at all.

She was just a wriggling ball of wool with
two little ears peeping out of the top!

15

By the time Mother Cat had untangled her,
it was time for lunch. Kitty stirred
a big pot of cream.

Splash,
splosh!

"Let me help you," said Mother Cat.

"No! I can do it by myself," said Kitty.

But Kitty stirred so hard and
so fast, she knocked the cream
right off the table.

Plop!
Oh, what a mess!

Kitty didn't look like Kitty any more.
She looked like a white, sticky, snow kitten.

17

Mother Cat took Kitty to the pond to get a
bucket of water. But the bucket was very big.

"Let me help you," said Mother Cat.

"No! I can do it by myself,"
said Kitty.

Kitty shoved the bucket into the
pond, and toppled in after it.

SPLASH!

"That's enough trouble for
one day," said Mother Cat.

19

But at that moment they heard a

grrrrrr!

and then a

woof!

The puppy next door had pushed his way through the hedge. Mother Cat scrambled up the nearest tree. Kitty stood still.

"Meoooooowwwwwwhissssssssss!"

Kitty hissed, bravely.

The puppy ran off back through the hedge.

Mother Cat jumped
down from the tree.
This time she wasn't
angry with Kitty.

"You did it!" Mother Cat smiled.
"All by yourself."

Yuck!

"**Yuck!** I don't eat peas," said little Mo.

"They are too roly-poly and way too ... **green!**"

Mo wished he could roll those peas right out of the door,

down the hill, and send them into
the river with a **SPLASH!**

"**Yuck!** I don't eat tomatoes," said little Mo.

"They are too squishy-squashy and way too ... **red!**"

Mo wished he could bounce on those tomatoes.

**Boing!
Boing!
Boing!**

Over the hedge and far away.

"**Yuck!** I don't eat carrots," said little Mo.

"They are too pokey-pointy and way too ... **orange!**"

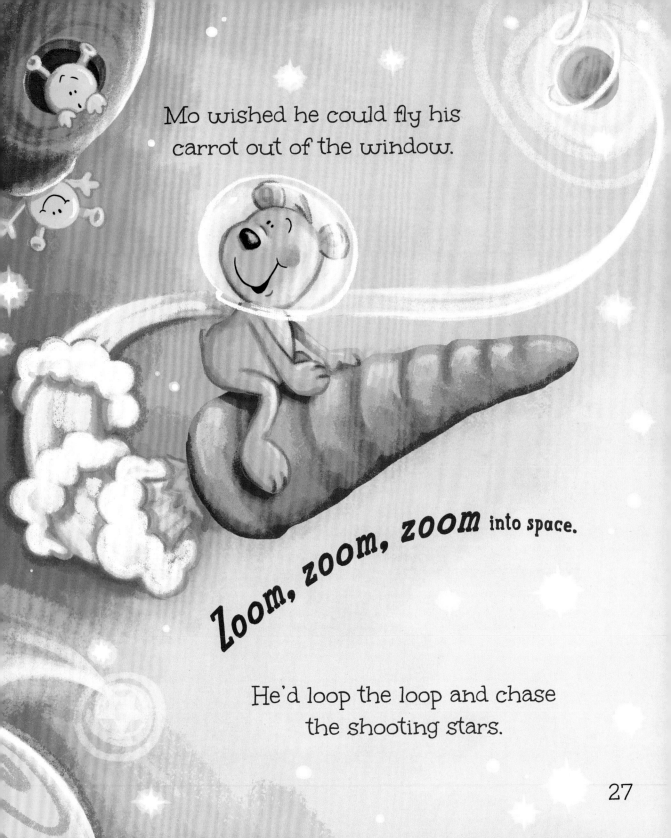

Mo wished he could fly his
carrot out of the window.

Zoom, zoom, zoom into space.

He'd loop the loop and chase
the shooting stars.

Then Mo started to feel rather hungry.
RUMBLE! GRUMBLE!
went Mo's tummy.

Mo looked at his plate. He poked at the carrot,
he pushed the peas, and he prodded the tomatoes.

A funny face looked up at him.
"I'll eat you up!" he thought he heard it say.
"I'll eat you first," giggled little Mo.

Munch! Crunch! Gobble! Slurp!

"Yummy, yummy. Time for pudding!"

I'm Big, Too!

Whoosh! went Leah.
Zoom! went Mia.

"I wish I could peddle,"
says little Freddie.

Dad runs after,
"You're fast enough already!"

30

Toot! went Leah.

Bang! went Mia.

"I wish I could play!" shouts little Freddie.
Dad calls out: "You're loud enough already!"

Chew! went Leah.
Lick! went Mia.

"Mine are all gone,"
cries little Freddie.
Dad smiles. "You're sweet
enough already!"

"Spider!" says Leah.
"Argh!" says Mia.

"Freddie to the
rescue," he calls
out loud,
Carrying the spider
to a bush, feeling big
and proud.

"You may be big, you may be clever and tall,
But I am THREE and I'm the bravest of all!"

33

The Magic Coin

Over the valley, up on the hill, is a neat, red
house, and in that house, beside the toy
box is a tiny, blue door, and behind that
door is an even smaller house...

Just the right size for a family of mice.

Snuffle!
Snuffle!

Little Mouse loves his home. But Little Mouse
dreams of adventure, of a world outside his
mouse house.

One day, when Little Mouse is exploring the neat, red house, he spots something shiny. A golden coin. Written on the coin are three magic words:

'MAKE A WISH.'

make a wish

"I wish ... I wish ... I wish I could explore a desert island!" Little Mouse says.

With a squeak, Little Mouse whizzes and whirls through the sky and lands on a faraway beach.

"My wish worked!" Little Mouse is so happy he jumps straight into the ocean. But he isn't the only creature in the ocean...

"Sharks!" gasps Little Mouse.
"I wish ... I wish ... I wish I was in a city!"

Little Mouse zooms through the sky and lands in a city with a bump!

But the city is busy. And noisy.

Brrrmmmmm! goes the bus.

Beep! goes the car.

"I wish ... I wish ... I wish I was high up in the clouds!" says Little Mouse.

Little Mouse flies up to sky.

"**Wheeeee!**" Little Mouse shouts out.

The clouds are soft and bouncy.
Little Mouse jumps from cloud to cloud.

Boing! Boing!

But storm clouds are gathering.

Lightning streaks
across the sky.

CRASH!

goes the thunder.

Little Mouse looks
down, and below him he sees a valley
and a hill, and on the hill is a neat, red house.

'I wish ... I wish ... I wish I could go back home!"
he shouts out, closing his eyes tight.

40

When Little Mouse opens his eyes, he sees all his things around him. His pincushion bed, his little swing, and all his toys.

Little Mouse loves his home best of all; over the valley, up on the hill, in the neat, red house, beside the toy box, behind the tiny, blue door.

Seahorse's Song

The sea is calm and the water's clear,
sea creatures gather around to hear.

The sun has set, the day's been long,
they're listening to the seahorse's song...

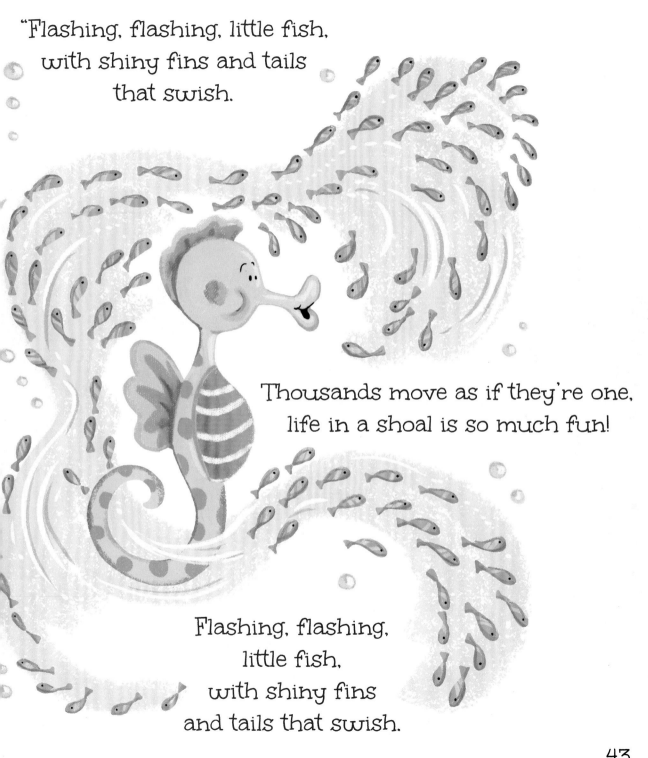

"Flashing, flashing, little fish,
with shiny fins and tails
that swish.

Thousands move as if they're one,
life in a shoal is so much fun!

Flashing, flashing,
little fish,
with shiny fins
and tails that swish.

43

"Glowing, glowing,
bright round moon.
Can you hear this
bedtime tune?

Shining light on ocean caves,
guiding ships through crashing waves.

Glowing, glowing, bright round moon.
Can you hear this bedtime tune?

44

Singing, singing, big, blue whale,
with giant jaw and thrashing tail.

Squirting water straight up high,
jumping under the dark, night sky.

Singing, singing, big, blue whale,
with giant jaw and thrashing tail.

45

"Pinching, pinching little crab,
a shell so hard and claws that grab.

Always moving, side to side,
plays in rock pools at low tide.

Pinching, pinching little crab,
a shell so hard and claws that grab.

Goodnight stars and goodnight fish.
It's time to make a bedtime wish.

Goodnight moon and goodnight whale.
Away to dreamtime we all sail.

Goodnight crab and
goodnight sea,
and goodnight you
and goodnight me."

47